About the Author

My name is Candice Samons and I'm a proud mother to my daughter, Taylor. She has been the inspiration behind the Taylor's Tales book series. Our journey with autism started when she was just 18 months old, and we hope to inspire others to embrace their differences and to accept everyone for who they are.

In this book, I wanted to focus on sensory exploration because Taylor and her friends have taught us so much about the unique ways each child experiences the world. Taylor is a sensory seeker, who loves making noise; she's often the loudest in the room, happily banging objects on surfaces. She enjoys exploring different textures and often puts non-food items like mud and sand in her mouth - she even once tried to eat a fly!

A central theme I want to convey in this book is that it's perfectly fine for children to explore their surroundings in their own unique way. The sensory spectrum is vast and every child navigates it differently. Some children thrive on loud sounds, while others prefer quiet and benefit from noise-cancelling headphones to help them cope with their surroundings. Similarly, some enjoy crunchy foods and gag at the mere thought of anything gooey, while others gravitate towards softer textures.

The characters in the book are inspired by the incredible people in Taylor's life who provide her with unwavering support and have learned to connect with her in her own world. I want to express my gratitude to all our family and friends who help us on our journey through the world of neurodiversity, and continue to be there for us every step of the way.

I hope you find as much joy in reading this book as I experienced while writing it. Always remember to celebrate your individuality and embrace who you are!

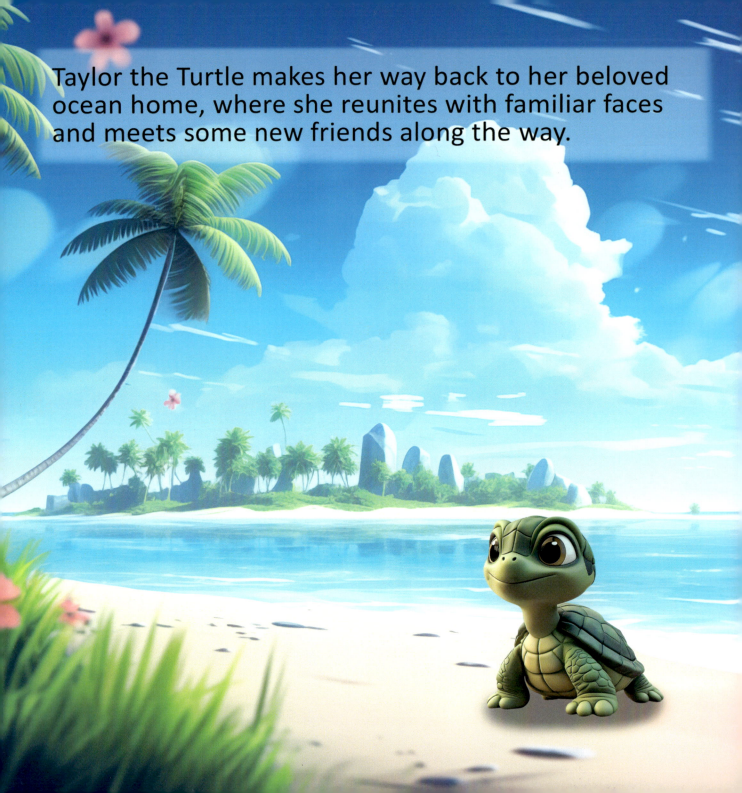

Taylor the Turtle makes her way back to her beloved ocean home, where she reunites with familiar faces and meets some new friends along the way.

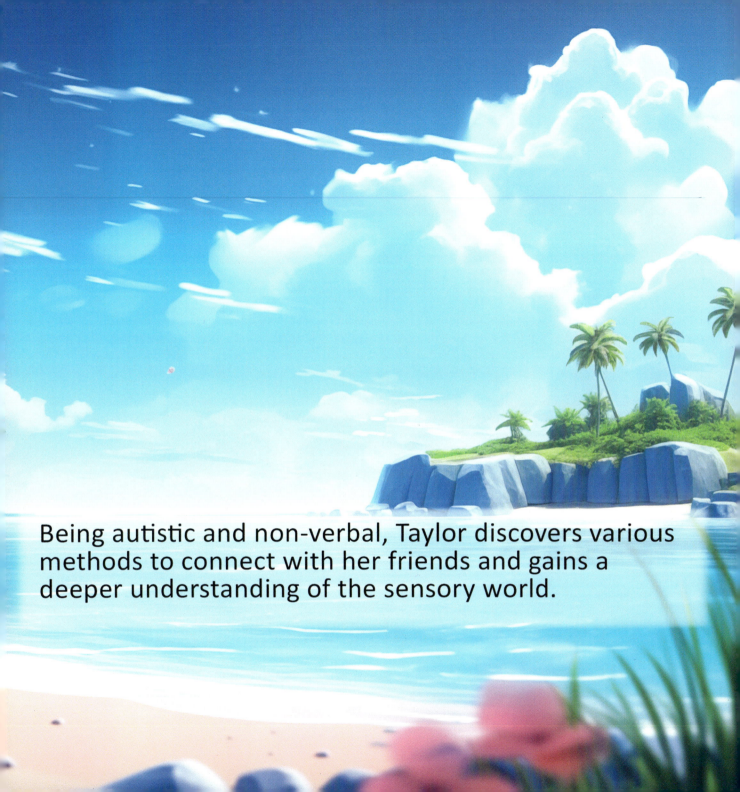

Being autistic and non-verbal, Taylor discovers various methods to connect with her friends and gains a deeper understanding of the sensory world.

Her first encounter is with JASON the JELLYFISH, who is JOYFUL. He shares his exciting quest to locate a lost treasure from a shipwreck. He asks Taylor for help, revealing that the treasure lies deep in the ocean, but he is afraid of the dark and prefers to stay where the light shines.

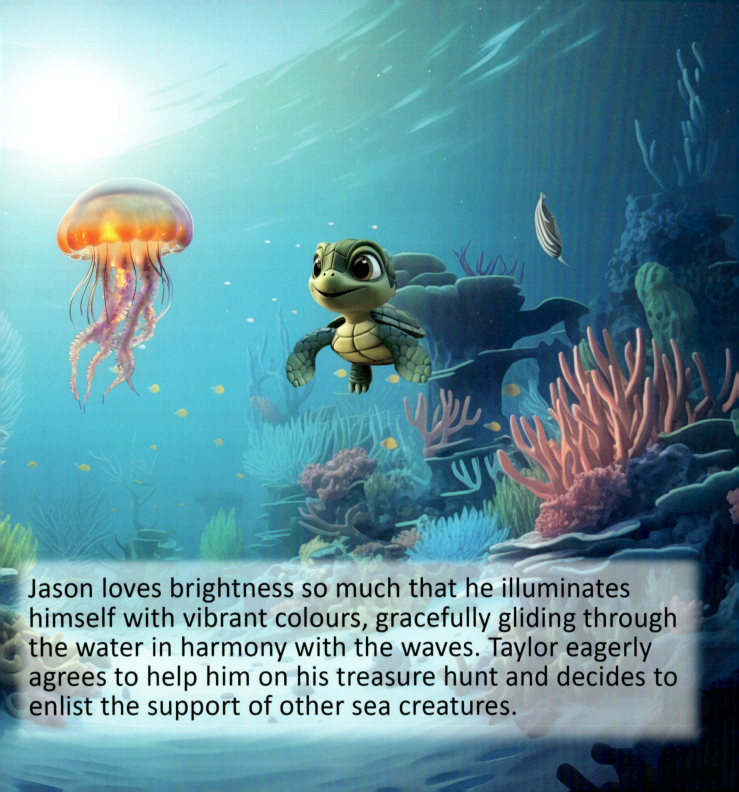

Jason loves brightness so much that he illuminates himself with vibrant colours, gracefully gliding through the water in harmony with the waves. Taylor eagerly agrees to help him on his treasure hunt and decides to enlist the support of other sea creatures.

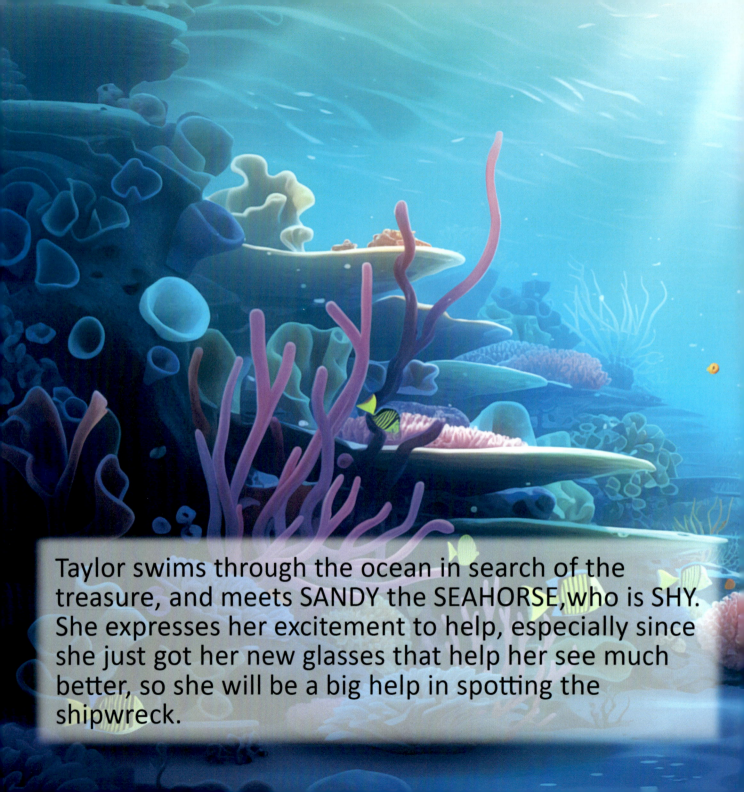

Taylor swims through the ocean in search of the treasure, and meets SANDY the SEAHORSE, who is SHY. She expresses her excitement to help, especially since she just got her new glasses that help her see much better, so she will be a big help in spotting the shipwreck.

Taylor learns that some sea creatures need a little extra help with their vision, and she's glad Sandy visited the optician, who checked her eyes and provided her with the perfect glasses.

While on the treasure hunt, she comes across OLLIE the OCTOPUS, who is OUTGOING. He is also non-verbal like Taylor so they communicate using gestures and sign language. Ollie shows Taylor how he experiences smell, highlighting his special arms that allow him to use his suckers to taste, smell, and feel the world around him.

Taylor describes that she is able to smell by sipping sea water and then expelling it from her mouth, using the sensory receptors in her throat to experience the smell.

The next ocean friend Taylor meets is NICKY the NARWHAL, who is NURTURING. She has a long tusk and can hold her breath under water for up to 20 minutes. She is quite particular about her meals and only enjoys specific kinds of fish.

Taylor learns that everyone has unique tastes; for instance, she prefers dry, crunchy snacks, whereas Nicky likes slimy treats, which Taylor finds rather 'yucky.'

Taking a short break from the search for the treasure, Taylor goes up to the beach and reconnects with her old friends, PETER the PENGUIN, who is PLAYFUL and SHEILA the SEA LION who is SPONTANEOUS. They teach her how different animals experience touch; Sea lions enjoy cuddling and resting against one another, while Penguins prefer their own personal space.

They have a blast on the beach, constructing sandcastles and splashing in the waves. Taylor shares her exciting quest to uncover the hidden shipwreck filled with treasure. Peter tells them about all his travels across continents, and some of the treasures he has found along the way. They have a wonderful time and they wish Taylor the best of luck on her journey.

Taylor jumps back into the ocean and meets DAVID the DOLPHIN, who is DARING. David had been having trouble with his hearing, which is essential for his communication, as dolphins use whistles and clicks to talk to each other.

Taylor learns about this unique form of communication, and that David visited an audiologist to improve his hearing. He was fitted with new hearing aids, so now David can hear all the sounds of the ocean and enjoy conversations with his friends.

As Taylor continues on her journey, she encounters CARMEN the CRAB, who is COURAGEOUS. Being a hermit crab, Carmen enjoys tranquility and prefers to wear ear defenders to block out the sounds of the ocean. When Taylor accidentally wakes her from a nap, seeking assistance in the treasure hunt, Carmen politely turns away and returns to her peaceful slumber.

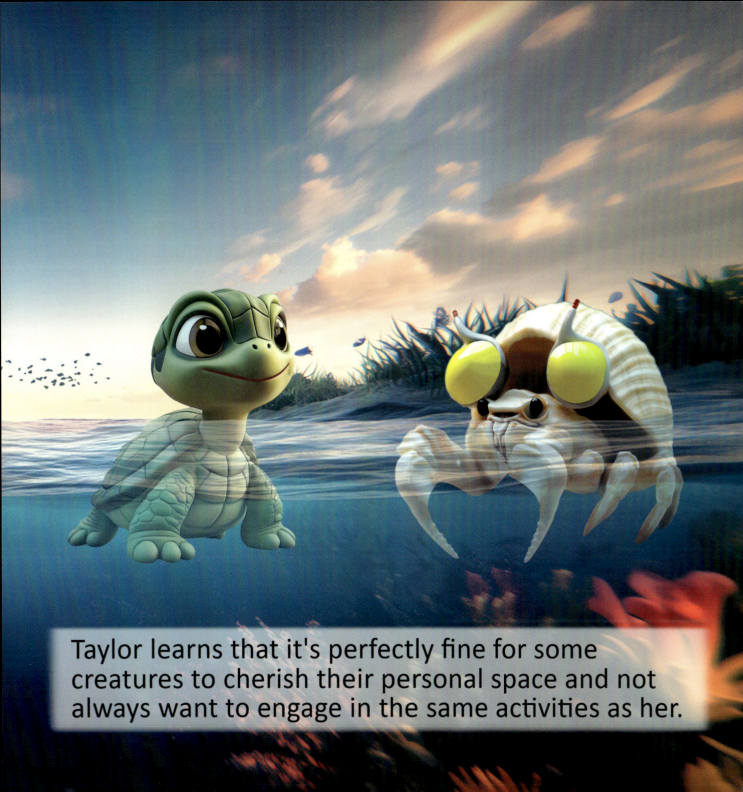

Taylor learns that it's perfectly fine for some creatures to cherish their personal space and not always want to engage in the same activities as her.

The final friend Taylor meets on her journey, is CHARLEEN THE CLOWNFISH, who is CONFIDENT. Charleen is adventurous and eagerly offers to help Taylor in her quest for treasure. She occasionally struggles to focus due to having ADHD (Attention Deficit Hyperactivity Disorder).

To help manage her energy, she performs flips and twirls while swimming. Taylor learns that Charleen uses movement as a way to self-regulate, similar to how she flaps her fins when she feels excited or anxious, a behaviour known as 'stimming'.

As Taylor's journey through the ocean comes to an end, she feels a wave of excitement. Thanks to her wonderful new friends, she has discovered the hidden shipwreck filled with treasure.